THIS BELONGS TO
PATRICK

G000160538

TEN GO HOPPING

First published in 1985
by Faber and Faber Limited
3 Queen Square London WC1N 3AU

Printed in Great Britain by
Jolly & Barber Ltd Rugby

British Library Cataloguing in Publication Data

Allbright, Viv
Ten go hopping
I. Title
823′.914[J] PZ7
ISBN 0-571-13473-4

ff

TEN GO HOPPING

Viv Allbright

faber and faber
LONDON · BOSTON

A little boy goes hopping.
One goes hopping.

1

A little boy and a grasshopper go hopping.
Two go hopping.

2

A little boy, a grasshopper and a mouse go hopping.

Three go hopping.

A little boy, a grasshopper, a mouse and a frog go hopping.

Four go hopping.

A little boy, a grasshopper, a mouse, a frog
and a rabbit go hopping.

Five go hopping.

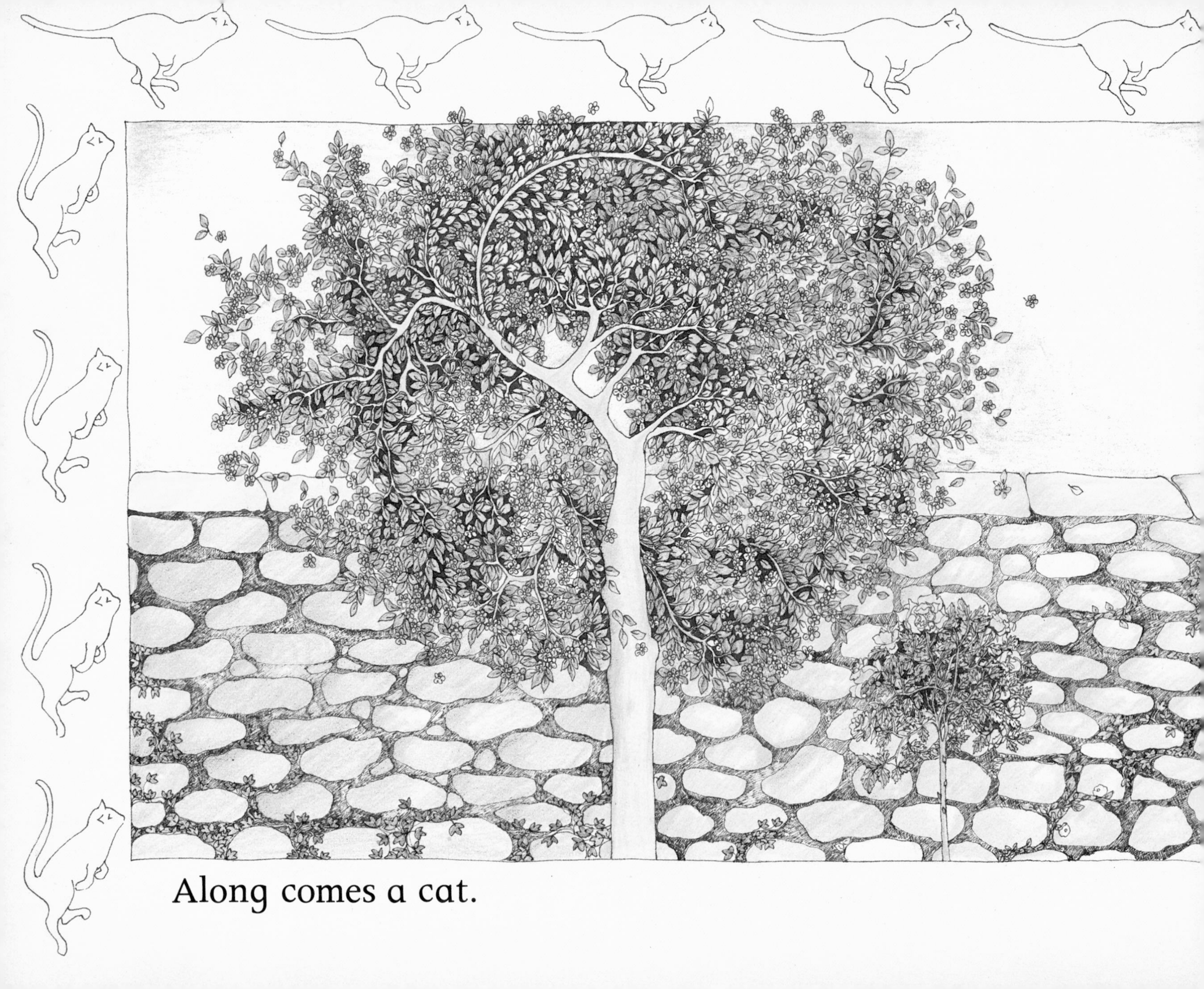

Along comes a cat.

A little boy, a grasshopper, a mouse, a frog, a rabbit
and a cat go hopping.

Six go hopping.

Along comes a dog.

A little boy, a grasshopper, a mouse, a frog, a rabbit, a cat and a dog go hopping.

Seven go hopping.

Along comes a monkey.

A little boy, a grasshopper, a mouse, a frog, a rabbit, a cat, a dog and a monkey go hopping.

Eight go hopping.

Along comes a kangaroo.

A little boy, a grasshopper, a mouse, a frog, a rabbit, a cat, a dog, a monkey and a kangaroo go hopping.

Nine go hopping.

Along comes an elephant.

A little boy, a grasshopper, a mouse, a frog, a rabbit, a cat, a dog, a monkey, a kangaroo and an elephant go hopping.

Ten go hopping.